The Rattlesnake Who Went to School

Craig Kee Strete

illustrated by Lynne Cravath

G. P. Putnam's Sons

Crowboy was going to school
for the very first time,
and he was afraid.

So when Crowboy woke up, he decided
to become a snake.
   Not just any old snake—a mean old rattlesnake
with very sharp teeth.

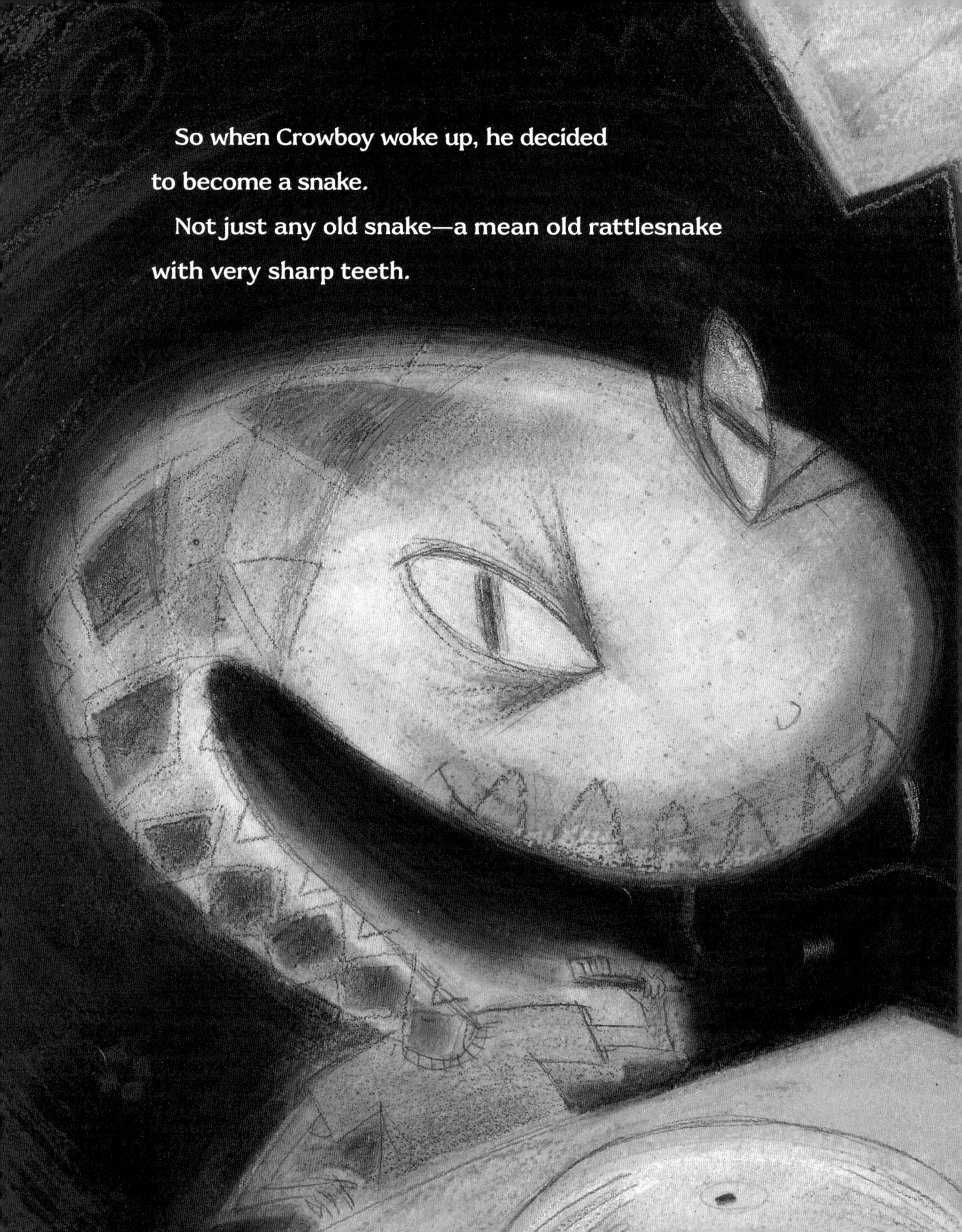

He crawled downstairs to eat breakfast in one smooth slither.

He wrapped himself around the kitchen chair and
stared unblinking at his corncakes. His sisters and brother
ate their breakfast, but Crowboy didn't.

Rattlesnakes don't eat corncakes.

"I'm a mean old rattlesnake," he said.

His mother ignored him. His brother ate Crowboy's
corncakes too.

"I don't care," said Crowboy. "I am only hungry for field mice." Nobody seemed to care that he was a snake.

Except his mother said, "Crowboy, stop sticking your tongue out at your sister. It isn't nice."

Ha, ha, thought Crowboy. I'm a rattlesnake. I don't have to be nice.

On the long bus ride to school, Crowboy crawled under the seats and tried to wrap himself around everybody's legs. Some girls screamed and some of the boys tried to kick him.

Crowboy didn't mind.
Snakes are used to kicks and screams.

Crowboy went into his classroom. The teacher looked at him and smiled. Ha, ha, thought Crowboy, she is afraid to get on my bad side because I am a rattlesnake!

But the teacher said, "Don't worry, Crowboy. You'll make friends."

Crowboy didn't know if he believed that, but a girl was staring at him so Crowboy reared up. He showed his fangs and pretended to bite her. The girl giggled.

Crowboy hissed angrily.

The teacher taught everybody to sing a song. Crowboy just hissed.

The teacher said, "Crowboy, stop hissing. If you don't know the words, hum along."

Rattlesnakes don't hum, thought Crowboy, and he rattled his tail.

In the cafeteria they had hot dogs, corn, mashed potatoes and greasy gravy. But no mice or tasty insects.

Crowboy sat by himself. Then that girl sat down across from him. She even smiled at him.

"If you're not going to eat that hot dog, I'll eat it for you," she said.

He handed it to her. Rattlesnakes don't eat hot dogs.

"I'm a rattlesnake," said Crowboy to the girl as she ate his hot dog.

"I didn't know rattlesnakes wore boots," said the girl, looking down at his feet.

"You're supposed to be afraid of snakes," said Crowboy, upset that this snake thing wasn't working out like he planned.

"I like snakes. It's spiders that give me the creeps," said the girl with a smile. "Thanks for the hot dog."

On the bus ride home from school, Crowboy stared out the window. He didn't blink once and he kept touching the window with his tongue.

At the kitchen table at suppertime, he slithered all over the place, but nobody seemed to care.

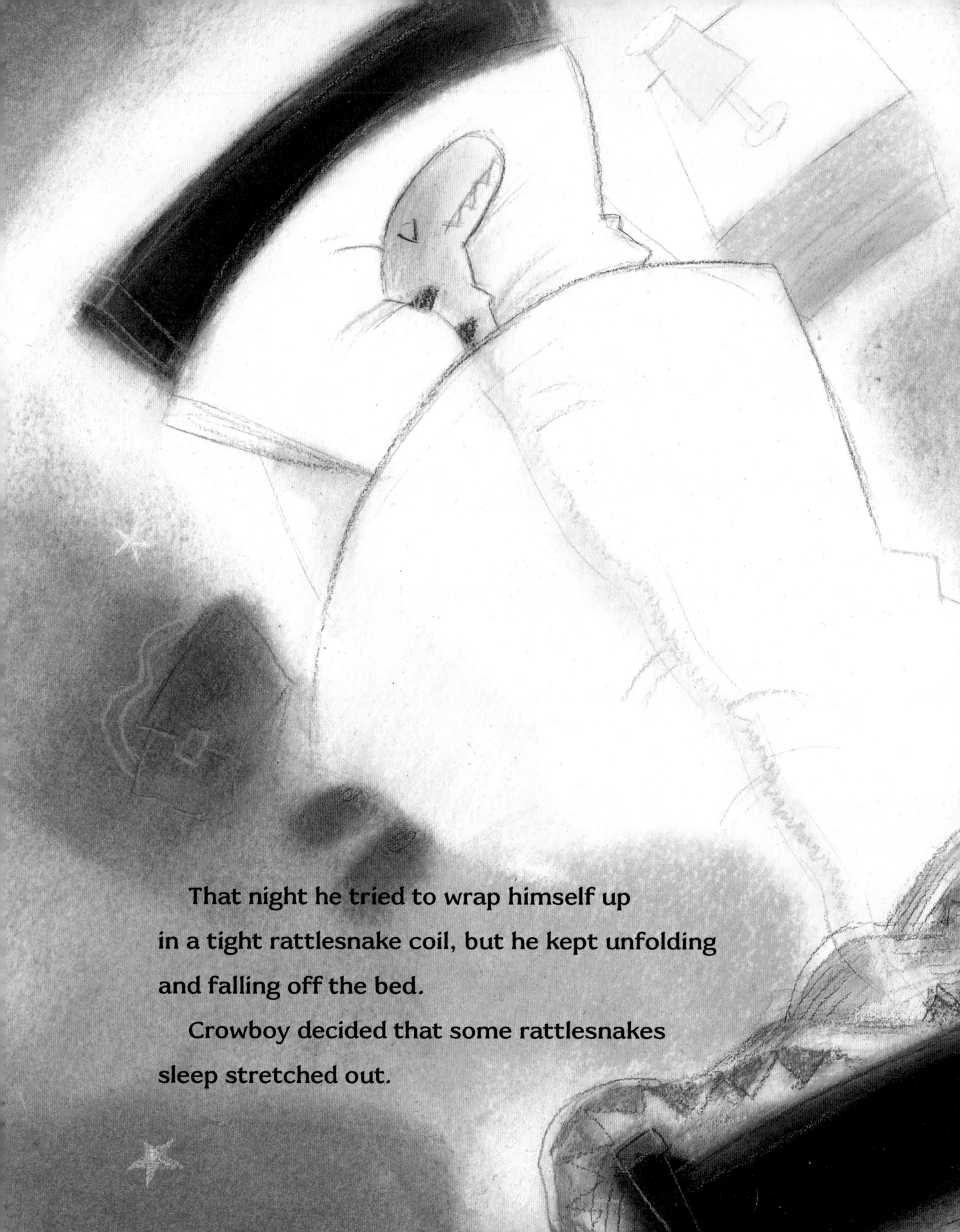

That night he tried to wrap himself up
in a tight rattlesnake coil, but he kept unfolding
and falling off the bed.

   Crowboy decided that some rattlesnakes
sleep stretched out.

On the morning of his second day of school,
Crowboy bared his big snake fangs and
checked to see if they were still sharp.

At lunch he remembered the hot dog he gave away. Crowboy was hungrier than a rattlesnake who hadn't eaten for a month. The girl who had eaten his hot dog yesterday stood in line beside him.

She handed him a small paper bag. "I brought you something. Just in case you get hungry."

Crowboy asked, "What's in it?"

"Something rattlesnakes love to eat," she said.

Crowboy looked inside. He saw a squirmy mass
of wriggling worms and big-eyed bugs.
Crowboy quickly closed the bag.
All of a sudden he wasn't
very hungry.

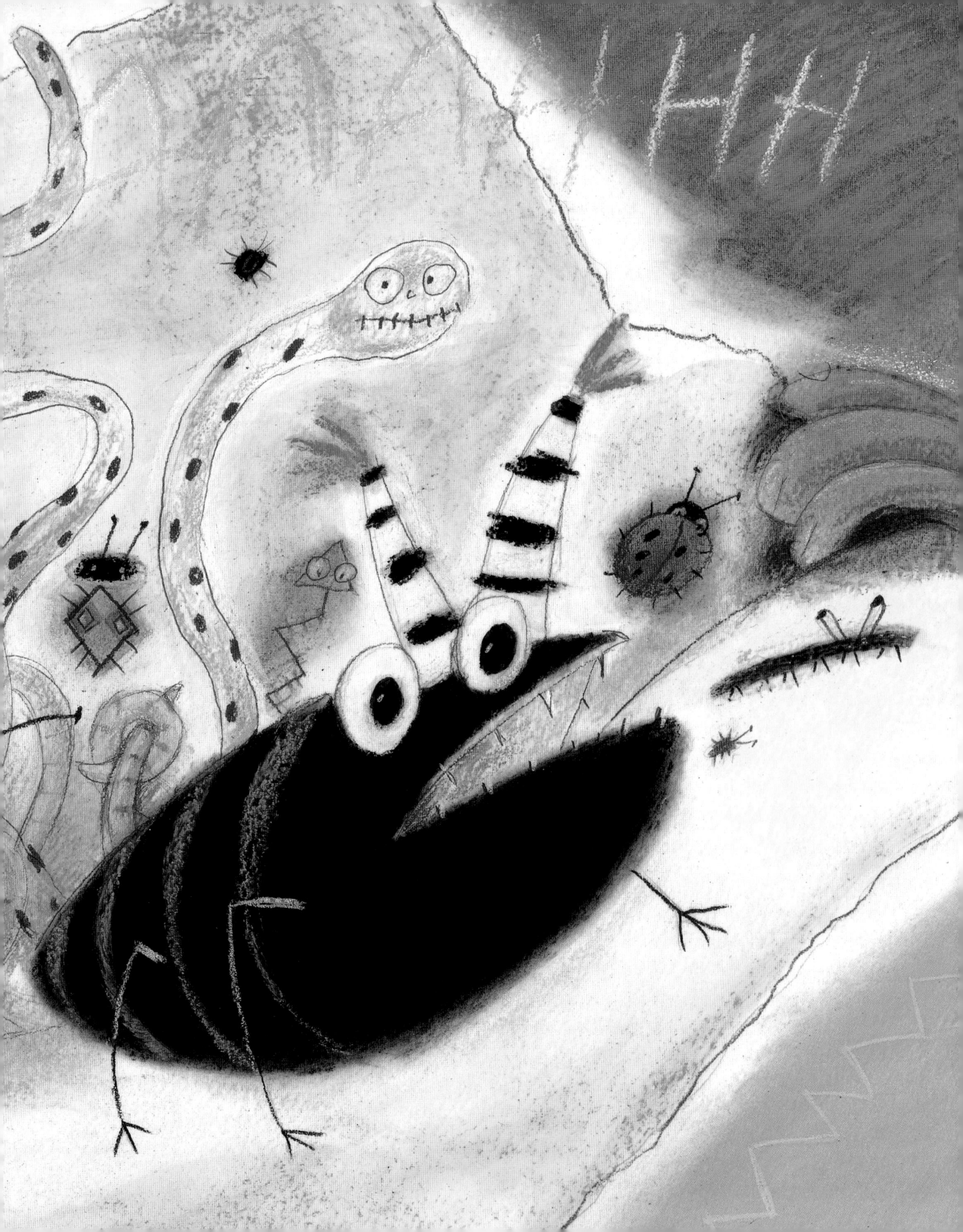

The girl asked, "Why are you a rattlesnake?"

"Because I don't have any friends."

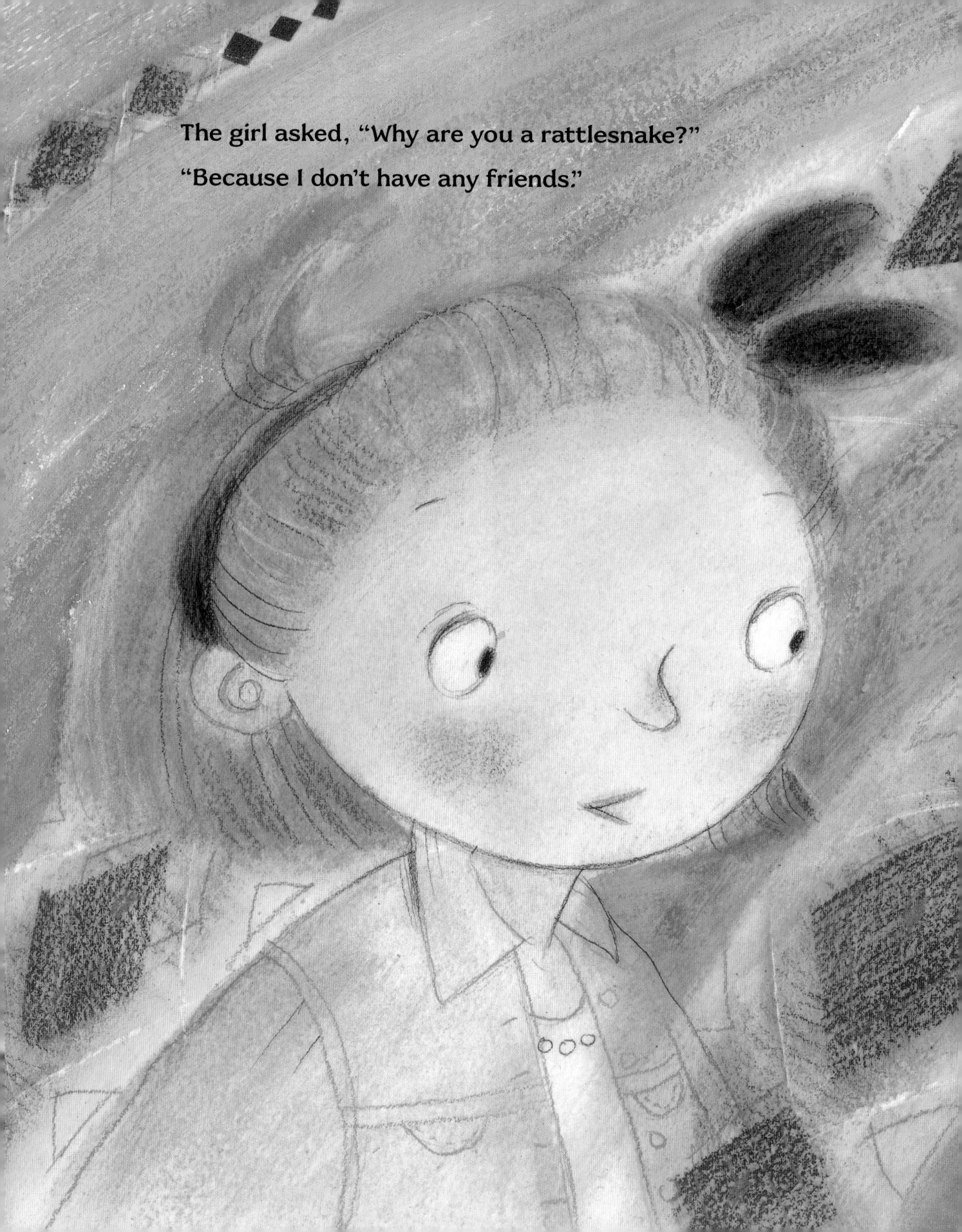

"You can be my friend," she said with a smile,

"if I can be a rattlesnake too."

Crowboy smiled the way no rattlesnake could smile.

"We'll be the kind of rattlesnakes that only eat hot dogs,"
he said.

And they slithered off together to the cafeteria.

For Jay —L. C.

Published simultaneously in Canada. Manufactured in China by South China Printing Co. Ltd.
Designed by Carolyn T. Fucile. Text set in Bryn Mawr.
The artwork was done in chalk pastels with acrylic medium on Arches watercolor paper.

Library of Congress Cataloging-in-Publication Data
Strete, Craig. The Rattlesnake who went to school / Craig Kee Strete ;
illustrated by Lynne Cravath. p. cm. Summary: On his first day of school,
Crowboy pretends he is a rattlesnake, but then he meets a girl in his class
who wants to be a rattlesnake too. [1. First day of school—Fiction. 2. Schools—Fiction.
3. Rattlesnakes—Fiction. 4. Snakes—Fiction. 5. Friendship—Fiction.
6. Indians of North America—Fiction.] I. Cravath, Lynne Woodcock, ill. II. Title.
PZ7.S9164 Bo 2004   [E]—dc21   2002004908
ISBN 0-399-23572-8
1   3   5   7   9   10   8   6   4   2
First Impression